This Ladybird Book belongs to:

BALFOUR

All children
have a great ambition …
to read by themselves.

Through traditional and popular stories, each title
in the **Read It Yourself** series introduces children to
the most commonly used words in the English
language (*Key Words*), plus additional words
necessary to tell the story.
The additional words appearing in this book are
listed below.

lady, goes, fairy, tiny, pretty, flower,
thumb, Thumbelina, happy, toad,
marry, son, leaf, swim, birds,
maybug, cold, dead, fieldmouse,
mole, tunnel, goodbye, dress

Ladybird books are widely available, but in case of
difficulty may be ordered by post or telephone from:

Ladybird Books – Cash Sales Department
Littlegate Road Paignton Devon TQ3 3BE
Telephone 0803 554761

A catalogue record for this book is available
from the British Library

Published by Ladybird Books Ltd Loughborough Leicestershire UK
Ladybird Books Inc Auburn Maine 04210 USA

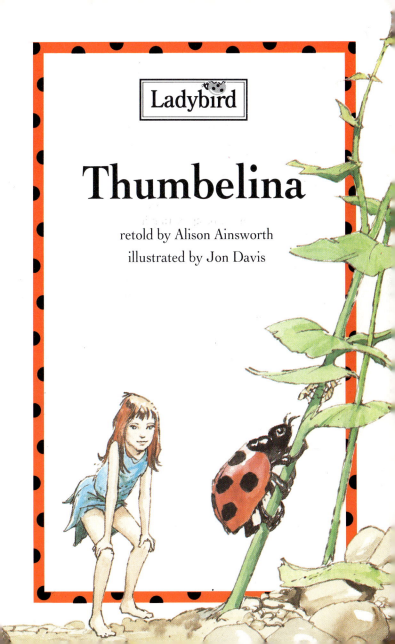

Ladybird

Thumbelina

retold by Alison Ainsworth

illustrated by Jon Davis

One day a lady goes
to see a fairy.

Good fairy, she says,
I want a tiny, pretty girl.
Can you help me, please?

Yes, says the fairy,
and she gives the lady
a red flower.

At home, the lady looks
into the flower.
She sees a tiny, pretty girl.

The lady says, You are tiny,
like my thumb.
You are Thumbelina.

Thumbelina is happy.
The lady gives her
a tiny bed, and tiny toys
to play with.

A toad comes to see
Thumbelina.

You are pretty, she says.
I want you to marry
my son.

The toad takes Thumbelina
to the water. She says,
Stay on this leaf.
I have to look for my son.

Thumbelina can't swim.
She has to stay on the leaf.

The toad comes
with her son.

He looks at Thumbelina.
Yes, he says, I want
to marry this pretty girl.

Thumbelina is not happy.
She says, I do not want
to marry a toad.

A fish sees Thumbelina.
Can I help you? he says.

Yes, please help me,
says Thumbelina.
That toad wants
to marry me.
I want to go home,
but I can't swim.

The fish says,
You do not have to swim.
This leaf is like a boat.

The fish helps Thumbelina
to go home.

This is fun!
says Thumbelina.
She can see flowers
and birds and rabbits.

Up in a tree, a maybug
sees Thumbelina
on the leaf.

He takes her up
to his home.

The maybug looks
at Thumbelina.
You are not a maybug
like me, he says.
I do not want you here.

Thumbelina goes down
to some flowers.

I can have this red flower
for my home,
says Thumbelina.

I can have apples to eat,
and I can play
with the birds
and the rabbits.

Thumbelina is happy
in her new home.

One day Thumbelina goes
to look for some apples.
It is cold.

I can't see any apples,
she says. She goes
to her red flower.
It is dead.

A fieldmouse comes to see
Thumbelina. I am cold,
says Thumbelina.
Please help me.

The good fieldmouse wants
to help Thumbelina.

Come into my home.
It's not cold, she says.
You can eat with me.

The fieldmouse has
a tiny home. She says,
You can stay
and help me here.

Thumbelina is happy
to stay with the fieldmouse.
She helps her.
You are a good girl,
says the fieldmouse.

One day a mole comes.
He likes Thumbelina.

The fieldmouse says,
I want you to marry the mole.
He can give you
a good home.

The mole says
to Thumbelina,
Come and see my home.
It's in a tunnel.

A bird is in the tunnel.
The mole says,
The bird is dead.

Thumbelina says, No!
He is not dead. He is cold.

Thumbelina gives the bird
some flowers for a bed.
She helps the bird
to get up.

One day he comes out
of the tunnel. You can
go home, says Thumbelina.
Goodbye, bird!

The fieldmouse helps
Thumbelina to look
for some flowers
for a new dress.

I do not want to marry
the mole, says Thumbelina.
I can't see the birds
and the flowers
and the trees,
in the tunnel.

Thumbelina looks
at the flowers and the trees.
Goodbye, flowers, she says.

She sees some birds.
Goodbye, birds, she says.

One bird comes down to
see her. It is the bird
that was in the tunnel!

Come with me to my home,
he says to Thumbelina.
You can see the flowers
and the rabbits.

Thumbelina goes
with the bird.
Up, up, they go.

Thumbelina can look down
on the trees.

Goodbye, fieldmouse,
she says. Goodbye, mole!

They come to the home
of the bird. Here we are,
says the bird.
You can get down.

Thumbelina sees
some tiny girls and boys
in the red flowers.

You look like me, she says.

The tiny girls and boys
are happy to see her.

You can stay here
and marry a tiny boy,
says one girl.

Thumbelina is happy. Yes,
she says, I want to stay.
This will be my home.

LADYBIRD
READING SCHEMES

Read It Yourself links with all Ladybird reading schemes and can be used with any other method of learning to read.

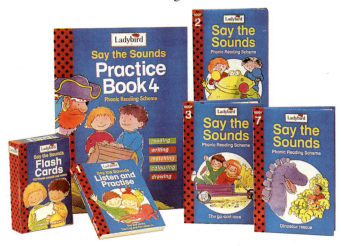

Say the Sounds

Ladybird's **Say the Sounds** graded reading scheme is a *phonics* scheme. It teaches children the sounds of individual letters and letter combinations, enabling them to tackle new words by building them up as a blend of smaller units.

There are 8 titles in this scheme:

1 **Rocket to the jungle**
2 **Frog and the lollipops**
3 **The go-cart race**
4 **Pirate's treasure**
5 **Humpty Dumpty and the robots**
6 **Flying saucer**
7 **Dinosaur rescue**
8 **The accident**

Support material available: Practice Books, Double Cassette pack, Flash Cards